LEROY POTTS
Meets the McCrooks

LEROY POTTS
Meets the McCrooks

by Vivian Sathre

illustrated by Rowan Barnes-Murphy

A YEARLING FIRST CHOICE CHAPTER BOOK

To those who listened and laughed, from Seattle to Los Angeles.
—V.S.

Published by
Bantam Doubleday Dell Publishing Group, Inc.
1540 Broadway
New York, New York 10036

Library of Congress Cataloging-in-Publication Data
Sathre, Vivian.
Leroy Potts meets the McCrooks / by Vivian Sathre ; illustrated by
Rowan Barnes-Murphy.
p.   cm.
"A Yearling first choice chapter book."
Summary: When Leroy Potts loses his memory after being struck by
lightning, the nasty McCrook brothers use him to steal for them.
ISBN 0-385-32192-9 (hc : alk. paper). — ISBN 0-440-41137-8 (pb : alk. paper)
[1. Robbers and outlaws—Fiction.]   I. Barnes-Murphy, Rowan, ill.
II. Title.
PZ7.S24916L37   1997.
[Fic]—dc20   95-53285   CIP   AC

Hardcover: The trademark Delacorte Press® is registered in the U.S. Patent
and Trademark Office and in other countries.
Paperback: The trademark Yearling® is registered in the U.S. Patent and
Trademark Office and in other countries.

The text of this book is set in 17-point New Baskerville.
Book design by Julie E. Baker
Manufactured in the United States of America
April 1997
10   9   8   7   6   5   4   3   2   1

Contents

1. A Yippee-i-o Kind of Day

"Yahoo!"

Leroy Potts was so excited
he danced a jig
through the cornfield.
He'd finally saved enough money
to buy that cornfield.
The farm that went with it, too.

That meant he could ask
Miss Hattie Mae Williston to marry him.
Leroy had been sweet on Hattie Mae
for as long as he could remember.
She was a right good cook, too.
If there was anything Leroy loved
as much as Hattie Mae, it was food.

Leroy mounted his horse.
He headed off toward the town
of Dusty Flats.
He was going to ask Hattie Mae
for her hand in marriage.

But suddenly a freak summer storm
caught Leroy by surprise.
It came on fast, starting with a wind.
In minutes the sky darkened.
It looked more like midnight
than midmorning.

9

Raindrops started falling,
getting bigger by the second.
Finally they reached
the size of chicken eggs.
Then a double bolt of lightning
came out of nowhere.

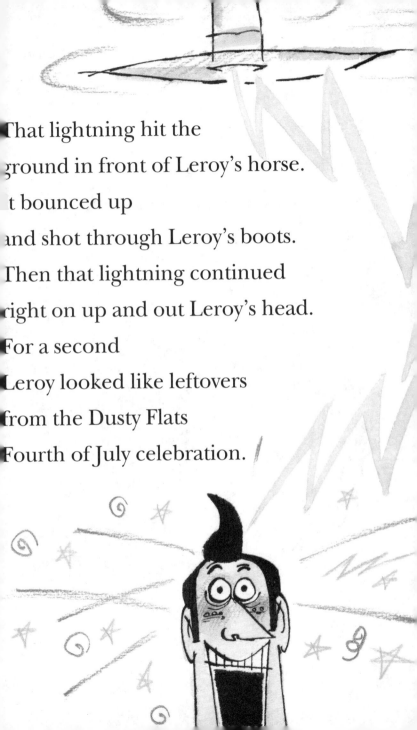

That lightning hit the
ground in front of Leroy's horse.
It bounced up
and shot through Leroy's boots.
Then that lightning continued
right on up and out Leroy's head.
For a second
Leroy looked like leftovers
from the Dusty Flats
Fourth of July celebration.

Quick as biscuits burn,
the storm was over.
The skies brightened
and the rain stopped.
But Leroy was a changed man.
Oh, he looked the same and all.

But when that double bolt of lightning
left his head,
it took most of his memory with it.
It was at that moment that Leroy
ran into the McCrook brothers,
Skete and Barney.

2. The Creepy McCrooks

The McCrooks squinted at Leroy.

"Howdy," Skete said.

"Good day, gentlemen," Leroy replied.

The McCrook brothers' eyes lit up like sparklers.

No one had ever mistaken them
for gentlemen before.
Right off they knew Leroy must be
a little flawed in the head.

And with every lawman around
looking for them,
the McCrooks figured Leroy
would be the perfect man

to do their dirty work.

"How about a game of Rob and Run? You can be first," Skete told Leroy.

Leroy scratched his head.

"I'm not sure I ever played before."

"It's easy," said Barney.
He tied a bandanna
over Leroy's nose and mouth.
"Now take this sack on over
to the restaurant.
Tell them to give you their valuables.
You got to look tough and sound gruff."

Leroy squared his shoulders.

He marched on over to the restaurant.

He opened the door.

Inside, the air smelled so good
his stomach rumbled.
It rumbled louder than
a volcano ready to explode.
For a minute Leroy forgot all about
the McCrooks' game.
Then Barney and Skete pelted pebbles
at Leroy's backside.
That made Leroy remember right quick.
Now what would be valuable
to a restaurant?

"Give me all your knives and forks,"
Leroy demanded.
"I'll take what's left of
that blueberry pie, too!"

The cook gasped.

But she did as she was told.

"Thank you very much," Leroy said,

tipping his hat as he left.

3. Biscuit Blunder

The McCrooks were not the least bit
impressed with Leroy's take.
But they did enjoy eating that pie.
"We'll give you another chance
at Rob and Run," Barney said.

The train will be coming through soon
o stop for water.
Those city slickers aboard will have
plenty of goods for a three-way split."
Remember, look tough, sound gruff,"
Skete told him. "And have them put all
heir goods in the sack. Fill it up!"

Just then the train came
around the bend, blowing its whistle.
Whooo—whooo!
As it slowed near the water tower,
Leroy pulled on his bandanna
and ran up to the train.
Just as he was boarding it,

25

his stomach growled like
a grizzly bear gone mad.
Made Leroy wish he hadn't shared
that blueberry pie
with the McCrooks.

Leroy noticed all the passengers
staring at him.
He was trying real hard to remember
what he was supposed to do.
His stomach growled even louder.
That's when Leroy remembered.
He squared his shoulders.
He held out his sack.
"Give me all your goodies, please!"
he said in a gruff voice.

Biscuits, chicken, cake,
apples, plums, and jerky.
Soon the sack was full
and Leroy's mouth was watering
like a canteen.
"Thank you kindly, folks," he said.

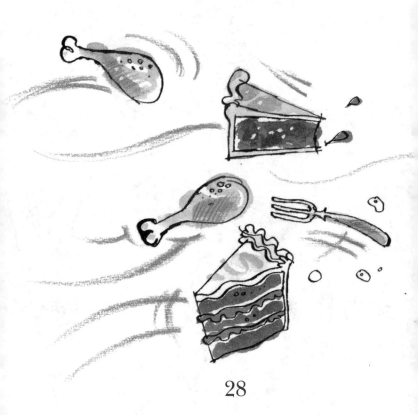

Leroy jumped off the train.

He handed the sack to the McCrooks.

When Skete and Barney peered inside
they got madder than
a swarm of bothered bees.

"This is how it is!" Barney buzzed.

"We want money!"

4. No Way Out

"We'll give you one more turn at Rob and Run," Skete said. "But this time you'd better get it right!

You can hit the bank
just before closing time."
Leroy finished off a chicken leg.
He thought the McCrooks' game
might be getting a bit rough.
"Why don't you gentlemen
play without me?" he suggested.

Barney sneered.
Skete glared so hard,
one of his eyeballs throbbed
like a heartbeat.
Right then and there, Leroy realized
he might not have a choice
in the matter.
It even crossed
his mind

that these fellows

might not be gentlemen.

"Get moving," Skete said.

He poked Leroy in the back.

"We'll be right behind you.

So don't get any ideas

about running off with the loot!"

5. Robbing the Bank

Leroy hurried to the bank so fast,
his bandanna slid off his face.
He pulled open the door.
There stood the prettiest little lady
Leroy had ever seen.
She smiled. "Hello, Leroy."

Leroy about turned to mush.
The McCrooks were watching him
from the shadows.
They didn't like the way
Leroy was acting.

'Get on with it!" they hollered.
Skete jabbed him on one side.
Barney jabbed him
on the other.

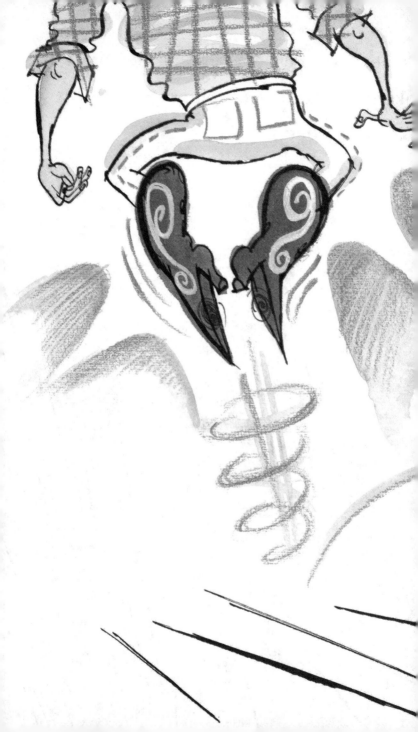

Leroy, being ticklish
as all get-out, nearly jumped
out of his skin.
As it was,
he jumped so high, he hit
the ceiling.
"YEOW!"
Leroy got a lump on his head
the size of a peach.

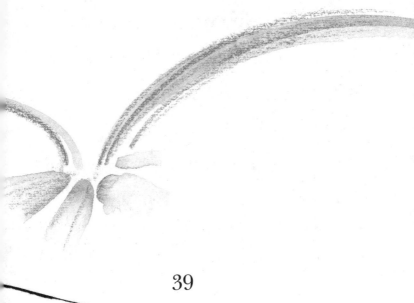

The good thing was, that bump
brought back most of his memory.
The prettiest little lady
he'd ever seen turned out to be
Miss Hattie Mae Williston.

The bad thing was,
Leroy was seeing triple—
three Barneys and three Sketes
were tugging on three purses
belonging to three Hattie Maes.
They were also yelling
at three bank clerks
to hand over the gold and silver.

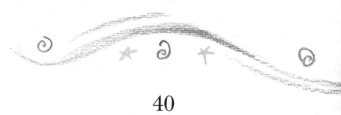

6. Leroy Bounces Back!

Leroy began circling all six
of the McCrooks.
But every time he tried
to capture one,
he just got a handful of air.

Leroy kept running around the
McCrooks, faster and faster.
Pretty soon he was so dizzy,
he started bumping into the walls.
Leroy ricocheted off those walls
like a bullet with a mind of its own.
That's when he banged into Skete
and Barney.

He knocked them
to the ground like overripe apples.
It was pure luck he missed
knocking over Miss Hattie Mae.
Finally Leroy's vision
began to clear.

That's when the sheriff dashed in.

"Good job, Leroy!"

He thought the robberies had all been
part of a plan Leroy had hatched
to catch the McCrooks.

"Here you go!" The sheriff tossed Leroy
a sack of reward money.

Leroy smiled and turned to Hattie Mae.

"Miss Hattie Mae, will you marry me?"

Hattie Mae nearly fainted dead away.

"Oh, yes, Leroy!"

"Yahoo!" Leroy shouted.

"I just knew this would be
a yippee-i-o kind of day."

Leroy apologized to the cook.

He bought all of her pies, too.

He sent them on to the next train stop

for the passengers he'd robbed.

Then Leroy rode home.

He never did recollect getting hit by

that double lightning strike,

which left him wondering about

those new holes

in the bottoms of his boots.

Vivian Sathre is also the author of *J. B. Wigglebottom and the Parade of Pets*. **She** lives in Washington state.

Rowan Barnes-Murphy has also illustrated *She'll Be Coming Around the Mountain*. **He** lives in England.